7. 21

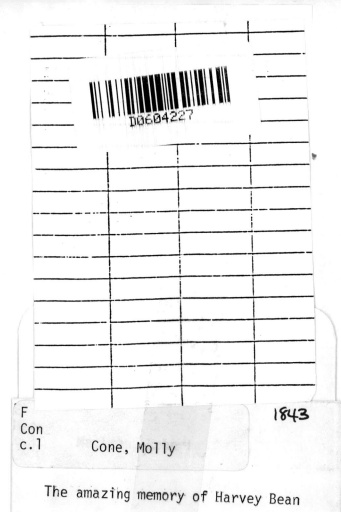

F
Con
c.1   Cone, Molly   1843

The amazing memory of Harvey Bean

Siskiyou County Schools Library
Yreka, California

The Amazing Memory
of Harvey Bean

E. S. E. A.
Title IV P

The Amazing Memory of Harvey Bean

MOLLY CONE

Illustration by ROBERT MAC LEAN

Houghton Mifflin Company Boston 1980

#1843

SISKIYOU COUNTY SCHOOLS LIBRARY

Copyright © 1980 by Molly Cone
All rights reserved. No part of this work may be
reproduced or transmitted in any form by any means,
electronic or mechanical, including photocopying and
recording, or by any information storage or retrieval
system, without permission in writing from the publisher.
Printed in the United States of America.
V 10 9 8 7 6 5 4 3 2 1

To Jerry who always remembers what I usually forget

Also by Molly Cone

The Amazing Memory
of Harvey Bean

1

"Harvey! Your socks!"

Harvey looked down at his feet. He didn't see any socks.

"What happened to your socks?" asked the teacher.

Harvey stared at his feet. He remembered getting up this morning and he remembered putting on his shoes. "I guess I forgot to put on my socks," he said.

The kids laughed.

The teacher sent him to see the principal.

"Harvey," said the principal without even looking up his name in the file, "I can't really say I'm pleased to see you. This is the fifth morning in five days that you've been sent out of your classroom."

"Is it?" said Harvey, feeling a little surprised.

"On Monday," said the principal, "you forgot to bring your arithmetic book back from home. On Tuesday you forgot your homework at school. On Wednesday you lost"—he cleared his throat significantly—"or *forgot* the assignment your teacher handed out. On Thursday you didn't remember that it was turn-in day for your extra-credit project. And today—now what is it today?"

Harvey looked down at his feet. "My socks?"

The principal sat up straight. "You mean Miss Campbell sent you out of class because of a pair of socks!"

"I guess she doesn't like bare feet," suggested Harvey.

"My guess," said the principal leaning back in his chair, "is that she is at her wit's end . . ."

Harvey looked up with interest.

"She has finally come to the end of her rope. The socks were the last straw, so to speak, the one that broke the camel's back, you know, and incidentally, her patience. Miss Campbell, you must understand, is, since this is the last week of the school year, rather short on patience."

"Patience," the principal repeated. "Do you know what we're talking about?"

Harvey scratched his head. It seemed like a long time since the principal had first begun to talk. Harvey's mind had wandered. He couldn't put his finger on exactly what Mr. Longworth had been talking about.

"I forget," he said earnestly.

And for no reason that Harvey could see, the principal laughed.

"Go home Harvey," he said. "Go home and have a nice summer. I'm giving you a half day extra just to save Miss Campbell's sanity. Though I'm not sure whether or not it's just a mite too late. Maybe I'm sending you home to save my sanity." He waved his arm toward the door.

"Clean out your locker, take all your stuff with you. Go home and have a nice summer."

Harvey hesitated.

"What's the matter?" said the principal. "I thought that would make you as well as Miss Campbell happy. Don't you know that there isn't a kid in school who wouldn't give his eyeteeth to be in your shoes, socks or no socks, right this minute! The sun is shining, the ice cream man is coming around the corner, the breezes are bringing good smells—what's keeping you?"

Harvey grimaced. "I just remembered—I forgot my locker combination."

A few minutes later, Harvey banged the door of his locker closed. He left inside the slip of paper on which the principal had written the combination of numbers Harvey had forgotten. He walked down the school corridor smelling the stale smells of scuffed vinyl floors, dirty plasterboard walls, hardened library paste, flowers wilting on book cabinets and crumpled Hershey bar wrappers hiding under desk tops.

Outside the schoolroom building, he followed the cement sidewalk past the rack of bicycles, stepped over the grape stain left by a melted Popsicle and the splat of dried apple core and crossed the front school grounds.

From the open window of his classroom came the slap of books being opened and closed, the rattling of paper, the voices reciting and the commanding sounds of the teacher's words.

His forgetfulness was the classroom joke. Harvey began to hurry leaving behind the snickers, the grins, the laughter and the hoots.

"Well, out of school already?" asked Mr. Hansen as Harvey passed his house. Mr. Hansen was retired. He spent half the day in his jogging suit walking around the block, and the other half hanging his legs over the hammock on his front porch.

"Yup," said Harvey.

"Guess it won't be long before you'll be crying to go back. That's the way it was with my Amy. Came dancing home on the last day of school—and the next day couldn't wait 'til school started again. You kids, you're all alike! What've you got to say to that, huh?"

Harvey clutched his stomach and made a vomiting sound and continued on his way.

If he never saw the inside of a school again, he'd be happy, he told himself as he reached his house. His mother's car was parked in the driveway, a little crookedly. The right rear wheel crushed the white rock-filled border. "Well, almost happy," he said.

He couldn't remember a time when he'd actually been happy. Not wholly happy, that is. Once his father had brought him a Pittsburgh Pirates baseball helmet which he'd won at a Rotarian luncheon meeting, the door prize or something. That had made him pretty happy. Once his mother had dropped him off at the Aquarium and had let him go in by himself. That had been fun and he had been almost happy.

Once his father had taken him down to the Science Center and once his mother had taken him on a ferry ride. But he couldn't remember being particularly happy either time because, in the first place, his father had stuck right with him, and in the second place, his mother hadn't let him stand next to the railing in case he might fall into the water.

The fact was, Harvey wasn't entirely sure what happiness was. No more than his mother or father did, though they were always talking about it. If it weren't for his father, his mother would be entirely happy, according to his mother. And if it weren't for his mother, his father would be happy enough, according to his father.

Harvey walked into his house.

In his bedroom he stood just where he had stood that morning when he was getting dressed while listening to the voices of his parents talking about their separation.

"What about Harvey?" his mother had said. "What are we going to do about Harvey?"

"What do you mean what are we going to do about Harvey?" his father had said. "Isn't he going to stay here with you?"

"For this summer I mean," his mother said, her voice scratching a little. "There's no reason why he can't just as well live with you for the summer."

Harvey had pulled on his jeans and T-shirt and then stood there unmoving through a long moment of silence.

"Maybe he'd better decide that for himself," his father said stiffly.

That's when Harvey had put on his shoes.

He looked at the floor near his bed. His socks still lay where he had left them this morning.

"Oh, hello Harvey." His mother stopped at his bedroom door. She didn't even notice that he was home from school early.

"Hi," said Harvey.

His mother had black hair and dark eyes and a mouth that used to turn up at the corners, and now was mostly down. She used to notice him a lot, thought Harvey. But the mother who stepped into his room, quickly straightened the spread on his bed, readjusted the window shades and started out again without once looking directly at him seemed like someone he had never met.

"Hey Mom."

"Yes?" Her face turned toward him but her eyes were glancing right past, over his head.

"You said I could decide."

"Decide what?" she said.

"About this summer."

She nodded though her head was turning as if she were listening for somebody else.

"Well, I've decided."

"That's good," she said absentmindedly.

"I've decided to go live with Dad."

Her eyes blinked and focused for a second straight on him. "With your father?"

"I thought I would for the summer," he said. "If it's okay with you I mean."

"Of course it's okay with me," she said too quickly. "If that's what you want," she added. It seemed to Harvey that she sounded relieved.

Harvey opened his top drawer and stood there looking at his socks. They were rolled up into tight little balls, hard like fists. "That's what I want," he said.

His mother reached out and patted his head. "We're still your mother and father even though your father and I have decided not to live together anymore."

"I know," Harvey mumbled.

"You be a good boy now." Her voice was softer suddenly. "You do just what your father says and—everything."

"Sure." He opened the door of his closet and

pulled out a duffle bag. "What are you going to do?"

"Me?" She seemed surprised at the question. Then she put her finger to her cheek and smiled. "Well, you can tell your father that I'm going to pack myself up and have myself a real vacation. You remember to tell him that."

Harvey didn't expect he'd remember but he nodded anyway. She stood there and watched him start to pack up his things. He could feel her watching him. He turned around and saw that she was gazing at his feet.

"You forgot to put on your socks," she said.

Harvey looked down at his feet stuck bare into his shoes and pretended to be surprised. "That so?" he said. "I guess I did."

Her hair swirled around her head as she moved impatiently. "Oh for heaven's sake, Harvey. You'd forget your head if it weren't fastened on."

Harvey saw himself sitting at his desk at school without his head and he grinned.

"It's not funny!" his mother said grimly. "Do you know you wrote down the wrong telephone number on your school card? You forgot the house-key when you went off this morning. And you didn't even remember to take your overdue books with you when you went to the library yesterday."

9

Harvey scratched his head. He couldn't even remember going into the library. It seemed to him that he had just walked around the neighborhood until he felt thirsty and then he had gone into a store to buy a bottle of Coke except he found when he put his hand in his pocket that he had forgotten to take any money with him.

His mother sighed. "Well don't forget to take your toothbrush."

Harvey went into the bathroom and got his toothbrush. His father's shaving things were already gone. So was the bathrobe that always hung from the hook on the bathroom door—and the framed photo his father had taken of Mt. Rainier that had hung on the wall at the stair landing, and the golf-bag that usually stood next to the front door.

He let his mother drop him off in front of his dad's office and watched her drive away. Then he went around the corner to the telephone booth and called his father.

"Dad?"

"Ahuh," said his father clearing his throat the way he always did when he talked on the telephone in his office. "Harvey? Is that you?"

"It's me," said Harvey.

"I'm pretty busy right now, Harvey."

Probably at his wit's end, thought Harvey. His smile reflected in the glass partition of the telephone booth looked like a big wrinkle on his face.

"I just want to tell you I've decided," said Harvey.

"Decided what?"

Harvey heard a flutter of paper as if his father had stuck the phone piece between his chin and shoulder and was using both hands to sort some papers on his desk.

"You said I could decide," Harvey reminded. "About this summer."

"Oh, yes—this summer." The sound of paper moving stopped.

"Well, I've decided to stay with Mother," Harvey said.

"I understand, Harvey." It seemed to Harvey that his father sounded rather relieved, too. "I just want you to know that I understand."

Harvey's hand seemed suddenly wet. It stuck to the phone piece. His tongue seemed to be stuck to the top of his mouth. He tried to swallow. "Well, I guess I won't be seeing you much this summer," he managed to say.

"As a matter of fact," said his father loudly into the telephone, "I've been thinking of taking off myself—maybe to Alaska, or somewhere."

11

SISKIYOU COUNTY SCHOOLS LIBRARY

"That'll be nice," said Harvey politely.

"Well, you can tell your mother I just might do that," said his father, sounding pleased with himself.

Harvey hesitated a moment. "Well, have a nice summer," he said finally.

"Thank you," said his father. "And Harvey—"

"Yes?"

"You too," said his father.

"Sure," said Harvey and hung up.

2

The man reaching into the supermarket dumpster didn't look hungry. His cheeks under the visor cap were round and pink. His short jacket barely zipped around his stout middle, and the small pickup truck on the back parking lot near the garbage cans looked new and red and shiny.

"Hi," he said to Harvey as he placed a sticky carton of cracked eggs and a bunch of black spotted bananas into a bulging plastic bag.

Harvey stood around and watched him sort through bruised apples, brown wilted peppers and dry wrinkled oranges.

"You going to *eat* those?"

"You cut out the bad part," the man said. "The rest of it is good as new. Here—" He tossed Harvey an apple.

Harvey caught it and turned it around in his hands. One side was bruised, the other side was crisp and perfect.

"It has to look good or it won't sell. If it doesn't look good, it gets dumped."

Harvey rubbed the good side against his pant leg and took a bite. The juice ran down his chin.

"Me, I can't stand seeing good things go to waste," said the man.

"Me neither," said Harvey, his mouth full. He ate all around the soft part and threw the core away.

The man looked at him approvingly and went back to turning over more garbage. Harvey climbed up to help him hoist out a box full of discarded tomatoes.

"Hey! Look what we've got here," said Harvey's new friend happily.

Harvey looked. "Rotten tomatoes," he said.

"Overripe," corrected the man quickly. "Just overripe."

A man in a white apron came out of the back door of the supermarket with another basket full of garbage. He started toward the dumpster—and stopped when he saw them.

"Hey!" he hollered at them. "What do you think you're doing?"

Harvey froze. He stood there, his hands glued to the box of tomatoes.

His partner raised his head and smiled pleasantly. "We're picking up some of the stuff you threw away," he said politely.

"Get outta here!" the grocery man shouted.

Harvey's friend gently set his end of the box down. He stood up straight. "There's no law against taking what's been thrown away."

"You get outta here! You hear what I said!"

Harvey jumped down from the dumpster. His friend slowly climbed down after him, then picked up the box of tomatoes and started toward his truck. Some of the tomatoes rolled out onto the ground.

"I'm not cleaning up any of your mess!" the grocery man shouted after him.

Harvey's friend grinned. He stuck the box down near the truck and went back and picked up the squashed tomatoes and tossed them back into the dumpster. Harvey stayed near the truck.

"And don't come back!" the grocery man shouted before he dumped his basket into the dumpster and strode back into the store.

Harvey's friend laughed. "I stop by here at least once a week. Most of the time he pretends not to see me."

Harvey wiped his hands on his trouser leg. He wiped his face with his arm. "Doesn't he ever call the police?"

"Nah! He can't. It's not stealing. You throw something away, you can't arrest anybody for helping themselves to it. You'd be surprised at the good stuff some of these stores throw away. Like these tomatoes." He bent to lift the box. Harvey helped him load it into the back of the truck.

"There's plenty there for both of us," the man said. "Take some home to your mother."

Harvey stopped helping.

"She can make some spaghetti sauce, or tomato soup."

"I'm not living with my mother," Harvey said.

"That's so?" The man didn't seem to think that was so unusual. "You living with your father then?"

Harvey shook his head.

"Well, who are you living with?"

"As a matter of fact"—Harvey chose his words carefully—"I'm sort of camping out for a while."

The man rubbed at his nose. Then he pulled off his garden gloves and stuck out a hand. "My name's Katz. Alex Katz."

Harvey shook warm pudgy fingers. "My name's Harvey. Harvey—" He stopped.

"Harvey? Harvey what?"

Harvey turned his head and stared into the back of the truck. It looked like a huge tossed vegetable salad. "I don't remember," he mumbled.

Mr. Katz didn't say anything.

Harvey said quickly, "I'm not very good at remembering things. For instance, this morning, I even forgot to put on my socks."

Mr. Katz laughed. "Well how about joining me for dinner, Harvey? My wife is a good cook. She likes to cook, even the things I bring home from garbage cans—though she won't admit it."

"We had tacos and refried beans for lunch on the last day of school," said Harvey eagerly as he followed his new friend into the truck. "One thing I really like is refried beans. Only not as much as fried rice. I just love fried rice. We had that once on the school menu. Just once. Last semester."

Mr. Katz glanced at him. "How come you don't seem to have any trouble remembering anything you ever ate?"

Harvey screwed up his face. He answered carefully. "Well, the fact is, some things are a lot easier to remember than others."

Alex Katz started the engine of the truck. "That's certainly a fact," he said.

3

Mr. Katz's house was the kind that people turned and looked back at when they drove past. It was the kind of house that made people open their eyes wide if they were used to houses that had regular windows and green shutters and white paint. It was the kind of house people pointed at when they looked back, and sometimes giggled at, and said, "Oh my!" or "Look at that!" It certainly was not the kind of house Harvey's parents would ever have lived in.

"Built it myself," said Mr. Katz proudly as he eased himself out of the front seat of his truck. "Built the whole thing. Would you believe it? Hardly cost me a cent."

Harvey stared.

"I like windows." Mr. Katz waved his arms toward his house.

He must have liked them very much, thought Harvey, because almost the whole front of the house was made of windows. Old ones. All different sizes put together. There were little windows and big ones and wide ones and skinny ones and short ones and tall ones and even a round one. And they were all fitted together like pieces in a patchwork quilt.

"Wow!" said Harvey.

"Found them, most of them," said Mr. Katz with a proud smile. "You'd be surprised what people throw away. Like I said, I can't stand to see good things go to waste."

Harvey stood there on the sidewalk and gazed at the wooden chimney rising at the side, and the shingles that started at the roof and went all the way down to the ground. Then he followed Mr. Katz up a cement walk to the front door.

"Dottie!" Mr. Katz hollered as soon as he opened the door. He shoved Harvey before him. "Look what I brought you!"

Harvey found himself in a barn-sized room. A black iron stove-fireplace stood by itself in the center. A stove pipe rose straight up into the highest

19

part of the ceiling. A staircase spiraled up to an upper loft. And a ceiling swooped down at an angle. Harvey rubbed the back of his neck.

"Alex Katz!" a voice shrieked from the back part of the room. "If you've brought home one more piece of cast-off junk, I swear I'll—"

Harvey turned his head. A woman in an apron was coming toward them. She was the fattest woman he had ever seen. She wore a scarf tied around her head and red tennis shoes on her feet. She talked as she walked and she stopped in surprise when she spied Harvey.

"His name is Harvey," said Mr. Katz, putting his hand on Harvey's shoulder. "This is Dottie," he said to Harvey. "She's not bad looking when she smiles."

Mrs. Katz made a face at her husband and then peered at Harvey. Her face creased itself into a smile. "Well, for heaven's sake," she said. "Wherever did you find him?"

Harvey's bare feet suddenly felt cold in his shoes.

"At the dumpster," Mr. Katz said with a grin. "Where else? I invited him for dinner."

"Don't look so frightened, boy," Mrs. Katz said as she reached over and lightly pinched his cheek.

"We're not going to eat you. Though I must say you wouldn't make more than a mouthful—"

Hastily Harvey stepped back. He heard Mr. Katz chuckle, and felt himself being pushed toward a big round table. It was set with two plates and two knives and two forks and two glasses.

"Don't mind my funny business," said Mrs. Katz kindly as she set another place. "I'm not much used to kids anymore. We had only one of our own and she grew up so fast I hardly got to know her."

"That's a joke," said Mr. Katz sitting down at his place at the table and spreading a paper napkin over his knee. He nodded at Harvey in a friendly manner. "That's supposed to be a joke."

Harvey smiled weakly. "My mother says funny things too—" he tried to remember when— "sometimes." It occurred to him then that his mother hardly ever said anything anymore that was supposed to be funny.

Mrs. Katz served dinner. It began with soup that had fluffy blobs floating in it. Harvey took a spoonful. The warm liquid slipped down his throat soothingly.

Mr. Katz said in a loud whisper, "If you want to please my old lady, all you have to do is eat!"

Harvey ate. He ate a lot. He ate right through the bowl of soup, the meat loaf with green pepper bits in it, the roast potatoes covered with parsley flakes, three kinds of vegetables that didn't taste one bit rotten, a bowl of applesauce and a large slice of carrot cake. It was a meal he wasn't likely to forget for a long time. Even though it did come from a dumpster.

Mr. and Mrs. Katz laughed a lot. They acted as if they liked having him there.

Harvey stopped eating all at once. He felt stuffed. He leaned back in his chair feeling his stomach smiling. And as he wiped his mouth with the paper napkin he felt his lips smiling too.

"I guess you'd better camp up in the loft room for tonight," suggested Mr. Katz. "It looks like rain."

Harvey yawned.

"Right this way," said Mrs. Katz and led him up the spiral staircase.

"I'll be leaving first thing in the morning," Harvey said through another yawn. They passed the open bathroom door. Glancing inside, Harvey saw soft pink towels hanging over the side of an old-fashioned bathtub.

The loft room was like an attic. The ceiling

slanted over a cot bed. In the wall was a round window. An old lamp had a fringed shade. A doll sat in a birdcage. A sewing machine was pushed into a corner. A basket was full of books.

"All this stuff here is Rat's," said Dottie, pushing the window open.

"Rats?" said Harvey, looking into the corners of the room.

"Our daughter," said Mrs. Katz as she plumped up a feather-filled pillow. "Her middle name is Ratmeyer. Because it was my name. We always called her Rat. Sharp as a tack," she said. "Could spell anything backwards."

Harvey heard himself laughing. He hadn't felt like laughing about anything for a long time. Rat. Ratmeyer. Mr. and Mrs. Katz. Carrot cake. It all seemed very funny to Harvey. Like something you'd find down a rabbit hole.

He washed his feet in the old-fashioned tub, and when he pulled out the big flat stopper, he stood and listened to the water loudly gurgling out. His home and the sharp voices of his parents seemed far away. He fell asleep smiling.

4

Harvey opened his eyes. Tacked on the inside of the closed door was a sheet of paper. On it were written some words. He stared at them, then yawned and rubbed his nose and sat up.

Sunlight came in through the round window, fell through the birdcage and landed on the bare floor. A piece of rug lay next to his bed. Harvey swung his legs off the bed and set his feet on the rug. He listened, heard nothing, then pulled on his clothes.

Before opening the door, he stopped to read the words on the paper tacked there.

One is bun, it said. Two is shoe. Three is tree. Four is door. Five is hive. Six are sticks. Seven is heaven. Eight is gate. Nine is line. Ten is hen.

Harvey grinned. "Some poet," he muttered and shut the door of the attic room behind him.

Harvey stepped down the hallway to the top of the stairs.

"One is bun, two is shoe . . ." The rhymes began to march through his head. Harvey tried to shake them off, but for some reason, they stuck and went right on stepping through. "Three is tree, four is door . . ." He went down the stairs one line at a time and reached the bottom on "Ten is hen."

An old table stood near the front entrance. Dented candlesticks sat on top of it. The front door was big and paneled and looked as if it belonged in a church. It had an immense door knob. On the floor in front of the door was a frying pan. A black iron frying pan.

A frying pan? What was a frying pan doing in front of the door?

A pot lid clattered, and a steamy rich odor reached Harvey's nose.

"Oh, there you are," said Mrs. Katz. She was wearing her red tennis shoes and her big apron. In her hand was a long-handled spoon.

"I guess I'd better get going," Harvey mumbled as he stepped over the frying pan.

"Oh dear." She sounded disappointed.

Harvey turned around and looked beyond the fireplace into the kitchen part of the house. A table made out of a half barrel and a door stood in the center of the kitchen space. Pots and pans hung from hooks in the ceiling beam. On the stove stood an orange pot and something in it was bubbling ferociously.

"Spaghetti sauce," said Mrs. Katz. "I'm making some of those dumpster tomatoes into spaghetti sauce." He followed her into the kitchen area.

"You might as well stay for dinner," she said. "If you like spaghetti."

Harvey remembered how nice it was last night with both Mr. and Mrs. Katz listening to everything he said, and giving him all those good things to eat.

He shook his head. "I think I'd better go."

Mrs. Katz stood in the middle of the kitchen. "Italian spaghetti," she said. "With Parmesan cheese and garlic French bread, and maybe—yes, I think so —blackberry pie."

Harvey hesitated. He watched her lift the cover from the pot and stir. The smell rose like perfume. Harvey took a deep breath.

"The milk's in the refrigerator," Mrs. Katz said. "Help yourself."

"Sure," said Harvey. He took a glass from a shelf without doors and opened the refrigerator door.

Harvey saw a bowl of cracked and sticky eggs, a battered carton of cottage cheese. Two huge bent cartons of milk sat on the top rack. He reached for the milk and stared. Not because the refrigerator contained a wealth of garbage finds, but because it also contained a letter neatly addressed, already stamped. It sat there, coolly, leaning against the damaged cartons.

"There's a letter in here," he said.

Mrs. Katz reached around him, took out the bowl of cracked eggs and set it on the table. "I never forget to mail a letter, if I stick it in the refrigerator," she said matter-of-factly. "I'm bound to see it first thing in the morning."

Carefully Harvey removed the milk, filled his glass, and replaced the carton in the refrigerator next to the letter. He closed the refrigerator door.

"I'll make you an omelette for breakfast," Mrs. Katz said, and began to open the lower cupboard doors. She searched for a moment and then stood thoughtfully regarding the shelves.

"The frying pan is on the floor in the front hall," Harvey said helpfully.

She smiled. "Of course. I put it there to remind me to remind Alex of a dental appointment."

"A frying pan?"

"Rat always used the frying pan to remind herself of afterschool appointments," she said, as if it made perfect sense.

"That's a funny way of remembering things," Harvey said.

"I know," Mrs. Katz said, not at all put out. "But it works. I hardly ever forget anything anymore."

Harvey looked at the table. It was set carefully with plates, napkins, cups, fruit juice—but no forks or knives or spoons. He grinned.

"You can empty the garbage pail," Mrs. Katz said to Harvey after breakfast, "if you want to help. It's under the sink."

"The garbage cans are out behind the garage," she called after him.

Harvey walked down the back steps, crossed the square of grass and emptied the pail into the plastic-lined big can. He carried the empty pail with him and walked around the garage.

It was big. Big enough for two cars and two more. It was big enough for two cars and one large truck, or two very large trucks, or even six very small cars.

But there were no cars or trucks in the garage. Mr. Katz's pickup truck was parked in the driveway right behind a small passenger car. As Harvey could see, there was no room for any car in the garage.

That's because it was filled. It held stacks of old windows, railings, lengths of lumber, doors, two-by-fours, piles of old bricks, old slats, old beams and old sinks. Stacked in one corner were one old stove, two toilets and three fireplace screens. In the rafters were laid wall panels and floor boards and I-beams. On the walls hung shelves of coffee cans and jars all filled with nuts and bolts and nails and screws of various sizes. And what wasn't piled on the floor of the garage, or sitting on the shelves, or hanging on the walls, or roosting in the rafters was spilling out the open garage doors, or leaning against the side walls, or was stuck behind the garage.

Mrs. Katz opened the kitchen window. "Whenever he sees something good that's thrown away he picks it up and brings it home. I've tried to get him to stop. But it's a regular affliction. He just can't bear to see anything go to waste."

Harvey peered into the overflowing shelter. Back in the corner he thought he saw the rusted runners of what appeared to be a sled.

"It's an awful mess," Mrs. Katz said as she came

29

out of the house and stood there on the driveway looking in too.

"Lots of good things in there," said Harvey, sure that he could see some round things like wheels back behind the sled.

"I suppose so," Mrs. Katz said, but it didn't sound as if she really believed it.

She tried to push the garage doors closed. But she couldn't budge them. Harvey tried to help.

"They're stuck," said Mrs. Katz.

Harvey viewed the situation. "It's only because the ends of those old boards are leaning against them."

Mrs. Katz peered in. "Or that old fireplace mantel," she said. "It seems to be leaning against the boards."

Harvey climbed over a pile of junk to see. "There's a piece of a stairway leaning against the fireplace mantel," he reported.

"He got that stairway out of the old Henry White Stuart Building when it was torn down," Mrs. Katz said, standing there with her chin in her hand and her elbow resting on the other hand.

Then she sighed. "Best not to touch it. Wouldn't do any good anyway. There's nothing in there that Mr. Katz would part with."

She picked up the empty kitchen pail and carried it with her back into the house.

Harvey stepped over some old boards lying on the driveway, and walked out to the front of the house. Across the street, a man was standing on the roof of his house with a broom, sweeping the shakes. He was sweeping just the way someone would sweep the kitchen. The man's hedge was neatly clipped, the trees in his yard were neatly pruned, the shades on the windows of his house were neatly drawn.

Harvey walked down to the end of the block looking at the houses on each side. All the driveways were clear and uncluttered, all the garage doors closed. All the windows matched.

A little girl was skipping rope in front of one of the houses.

"Hi," she said and stopped jumping to stare at him curiously. "You don't live around here."

Harvey grimaced at her. "Visiting," he said and started to walk past.

She blocked his way. "Who you visiting?"

He told himself he didn't have to answer if he didn't want to. "Some people up there," he mumbled, jerking his head toward the upper end of the street.

"You don't mean the crazy house!" she said and flung her hair out of her eyes. "My mother won't even let me walk past that house."

Harvey tried to ignore her. He tried walking on, but her voice came after him.

"My mother says they're a disgrace to the neighborhood. She says if they don't get busy and clean up the junk lying all over their yard, she's going to complain to the city. She says their place looks like the city dump . . ."

Harvey began to run. He ran for three blocks before he slowed down to a walk again. He walked past the supermarket looking straight ahead, hoping that no one would think he was the same boy who helped Mr. Katz take garbage from the dumpster the day before. He walked all the way to a shopping mall. He was standing there considering whether to go into Pizza Pete's for a pizza or just to get a hamburger at the place across the way when he saw his mother coming down the mall toward him. She was walking with her arms full of packages, looking at the displays in the windows. When she turned her head she would see him.

Harvey whirled around, bounded into the pizza shop and skidded to the end of the far line, keeping his eyes on the entrance. His mother sailed past.

"Your order please?"

Harvey turned around. "What?"

"Your order?" said the girl in a striped hat, standing behind the counter.

"Oh." Harvey looked vaguely around.

"We have mushroom with chopped olives and mozzarella cheese. Pepperoni, anchovies and tomatoes. Salami, pineapple . . ."

"I'm not hungry," Harvey mumbled and moved out of the line. He heard someone laugh as he went slowly toward the entrance and peered out before he bounded out and headed the other way.

He kept glancing back over his shoulder as he ran across the parking lot and several blocks more. When he came to a supermarket, he went around behind the store, avoiding the customer parking lot.

"Hey, Harvey!"

Harvey stopped. Slowly he turned around.

Hailing him was Mr. Katz, standing, both feet firmly planted in rotten vegetables, atop a dumpster.

"Come over here and give me a hand," hollered Mr. Katz.

Harvey moved toward him. He helped Mr. Katz lift a box full of dented cans down and helped him carry it to his truck.

"Hop in," Mr. Katz said, holding the door open

and fumbling in his blazer pocket for his car keys. "I'll give you a ride home."

Slowly Harvey climbed in. He hadn't intended to go back to the Katz house.

"Lucky I ran into you," Mr. Katz said. He started the engine and winked at Harvey.

And in no time at all the red truck was clattering up the neat street, past the house where the little girl had been jumping rope that morning, past the freshly swept shake roof and back into the cluttered driveway of the crazy house.

5

That night Harvey dreamed he was walking down the street and saw his mother coming toward him and she walked right past him without even turning her head.

Harvey opened his eyes with his heart thumping wildly and saw the moonlight coming through the round window and the old doll grinning at him from inside the birdcage. She was grinning at him like the little girl down the block. Harvey squeezed his eyes shut so he wouldn't have to see the doll face and fell asleep again. This time he dreamed he started off to school and got there late because he had forgotten where the school was.

When he woke up in the morning, Harvey heard the sound of voices arguing and thought at first he was back in his own bed at home. It took him a little while to realize that the voices belonged to Mr. and Mrs. Katz and not to his parents. They were arguing about all the rotten food Mr. Katz kept bringing home from the dumpsters. And about all the junk piling up in the garage and spilling out onto the driveway.

Harvey looked past the doll in the birdcage at the poem tacked to his door. One is bun. Two is shoe . . . He frowned.

He thought of all the different-sized windows in the front wall of the house. And the refrigerator full of rotten food. He thought of the letter in the refrigerator and the frying pan on the front hall floor. Then, quickly, he jumped out of bed, gathered his things, pulled on his clothes, and shut the door behind him.

Mr. Katz's red truck was gone. Mrs. Katz was sitting with a bowl of half-rotting apples on her lap. She was peeling each one and cutting out the brown part and putting the other part in a big bowl. Beside her stood a box of potatoes, not very good looking potatoes. There were rotten spots in them too.

"We're having potato pancakes for dinner," she said happily. "And applesauce for dessert. Don't you just love potato pancakes and applesauce?"

Harvey stood there and watched her take a bowl full of apple chunks and drop them into a big pot simmering on the stove. It occurred to him that Mrs. Katz liked to argue. She liked to argue almost as much as she loved to cook. She liked to cook just as much as Mr. Katz liked to find things that were too good to waste. Mrs. Katz picked up a wooden spoon and stirred. A sweet cinnamon smell rose and drifted around Harvey's head.

"If you want to do something for me today"— Mrs. Katz was smiling at him—"you could go get my new glasses at the optometrist's. They're supposed to be ready for me today."

"All right," Harvey heard himself say.

"All you have to do is take the bus on the corner and go to 1453 Main Street."

Harvey hesitated. He wasn't very good at remembering numbers.

"It's easy to remember," she said. "Just think—I love apple pie."

"You want me to get some apple pie?"

"Not *get* it, *think* it," she said. "Think—I love apple pie. 1 4 5 3. The numbers equal the number of letters in each word."

Harvey grinned. "I love apple pie," he said, and in his head counted the letters in each word: 1 4 5 3.

"On Main Street," she said. "My aunt is nuts."

Harvey stared at her. "You mean your aunt lives there?"

"So you won't forget the name of the street," Mrs. Katz explained patiently. "Think—*My Aunt Is Nuts.* The first letter of each word—put together they spell M-A-I-N. Main Street."

"I love apple pie. My aunt is nuts," said Harvey as he hopped onto the bus at the corner.

"What?" said the conductor.

"Nothing," said Harvey, and took a seat.

An old man sitting on the front seat tapped the bus driver on the shoulder, rolled his eyes toward Harvey, and tapped at his forehead.

Harvey squinched down in his seat. "I love apple pie. My aunt is nuts," he kept muttering to himself. He watched the street signs sliding past.

"Maple," called the conductor.

My Aunt Is Nuts. "Main," Harvey said. "I want Main."

The conductor grinned at him. "No you don't. You want Maple. All the street names around here were changed to names of trees yesterday."

Harvey sat there looking blankly out.

"Well, you going to get out?"

Harvey jumped off. "I love apple pie," he said as he looked up and down the street.

"The bakery is right across the street," a woman waiting for another bus said. "But they only bake pies on Wednesday, I think."

"Thanks," said Harvey. He waited until she had boarded her bus before he went into the little shop with 1453 on the window.

On the way back, the bus stopped near his old school. And before Harvey even thought about it, he had jumped off. He walked around the empty building. A back entrance door was propped open and he could see stacks of kindergarten-sized chairs piled in the middle of the hallway.

A man in a pair of white overalls carrying a carton came down the hall toward him. The man stopped when he saw Harvey. "School's closed!" he hollered.

Harvey hollered back, "I don't care if it is!" and ran to the corner and hopped onto a bus again.

"You have any trouble?" Mrs. Katz asked when Harvey finally returned with the new glasses.

"Nope." He handed her the small package.

Mrs. Katz took out her new glasses, put them on her nose and gazed at Harvey. "I'd better let the seam out in your pants," she said.

"Hi," said Mr. Katz, coming in and sitting down at the kitchen table. He opened the newspaper to the funny pages.

"Hi," said Harvey, and then said to Mrs. Katz, "By the way, your aunt isn't nuts anymore."

"What?"

"She Peels Lemons Elegantly. Since yesterday," he added. "They changed the name of the street."

Mrs. Katz was frowning. "Maple—I hope I remember that," she said.

Harvey opened the refrigerator and pushed away a new letter to get at the milk. He poured himself a glassful and gulped it all down.

"You could think syrup," he suggested.

"Well, that's so!" said Mrs. Katz, looking at Harvey with pleased surprise. "I never thought of that."

Mr. Katz glanced up from his funny pages. "I can't make heads or tails out of what you two are talking about." He eyed them suspiciously.

"That's because you don't listen," said Mrs. Katz promptly. "Now, Harvey listens. Harvey's a good listener."

"I am?" said Harvey.

"You'd understand perfectly if you bothered to listen," Mrs. Katz continued to her husband.

"What do you mean I don't listen?" said Mr. Katz, letting the newspaper slip to the floor.

Harvey scrambled under the table to get it.

"I mean bringing home more cracked eggs when I've just told you we've got a refrigerator full. Or dragging home pieces of old fence when the whole neighborhood is complaining about the stuff you've already got stacked in the garage and sitting on the driveway."

"Who's complaining!" demanded Mr. Katz. "I don't hear any complaints."

Mrs. Katz nodded. "That's exactly what I said," she said. "You don't listen."

Grinning, Harvey set the sheet of newspaper on the table. He grinned every time he thought about it. That night, in his attic bed, he lay there with his hands propped behind his head, grinning and thinking.

He thought about the funny windows, and the frying pan, and the letter in the refrigerator, and about all the stuff Mr. Katz kept bringing home from the dumpsters for Mrs. Katz to cook, and the garage full of junk, and Mrs. Katz's nutty numbering system. Harvey laughed. He laughed out loud. The doll in the birdcage stared at him. Harvey looked at the doll and thought of the little girl down the street. *Crazy house.*

"Oh, go jump your rope!" he shouted at the grinning face, and sticking his nose into his pillow he went to sleep.

6

The first thing Harvey saw the next morning when he looked out of his round window was a strange person poking around the neighborhood. He ducked when the man glanced up toward his window, then he dressed fast and dashed down the stairs.

"Help yourself to the fruit sauce," said Mrs. Katz. "It's pear and apple and green grapes and some banana and a little orange and a nice ripe papaya."

"You want me to help you go to the dumpster?" he said eagerly as soon as Mr. Katz reached for his visor cap.

Mr. Katz smiled. "Well, now, that would be a great help."

"Don't bring me any more eggs!" hollered Mrs. Katz. They climbed into the red truck.

As they backed down the driveway, Harvey bent his head to his knees, pretending to be tying his shoe. The strange man's car was parked across the street and he was sitting in it flipping pages of a notebook.

"Harvey?"

Harvey raised his head, saw they had turned the corner and sat up. "Yes?"

Mr. Katz was paying close attention to his driving. "Mrs. Katz and me, we'd sure like to meet your folks."

He hadn't even noticed the strange man snooping around outside his house, thought Harvey. He smiled confidently. "They're not back yet."

Mr. Katz flicked him with a glance. "They gone someplace?"

"Separate vacations," Harvey said, thinking quickly. He began to talk fast, his voice a little loud. "That's what we all decided to do this year—take separate vacations. My mom, she just decided to pack herself up and take a real vacation. And my dad, well he decided to go off to Alaska, or someplace like that. Soon as they get where they're going they'll probably send me postcards."

Mr. Katz gave a funny little laugh. "Separate vacations," he said. "That's a new style for me. Everybody going every which way." He wagged his head.

44

"It's a funny world, all right. Sometimes Dottie and me, we look around and wonder if everybody but us hasn't gone a mite crazy." Mr. Katz turned into a supermarket back lot. "Depends on how you look at it, I guess. Everybody looks at things differently —if you know what I mean." He drove right up to the biggest dumpster, stopped the car and opened the door.

Harvey couldn't help thinking of the Katzes' neighbors. *Crazy house.* He tried not to grin. "I know what you mean," he said, as he climbed up into the dumpster after Mr. Katz.

Suddenly Harvey began to feel pretty good. He didn't care what anybody else thought. He liked staying with Mr. and Mrs. Katz. He liked eating pear-apple-green grape-banana-orange-papaya sauce. He liked eating omelettes made of dumpster eggs, and pancakes made of dumpster flour. He even liked helping Mr. Katz.

He helped haul out a whole box full of dented cans of vegetables. He spotted a whole gallon carton of sour milk. He began to enjoy himself. Instead of black spotted bananas he fancied he saw a mile-high banana cake. And when he pulled out a soft overripe pineapple, he could actually smell the enticing aroma of pineapple upside-down cake.

In spite of the man snooping around the neighborhood that morning, it would have been a Grade A perfect day if Mr. Katz's horn hadn't got itself stuck and started honking, and the supermarket manager hadn't come out and lost his temper and begun to chase them, and Mr. Katz hadn't slipped on a squashed avocado and bumped his head on the dumpster lid and twisted his ankle.

Mr. Katz ate his dinner with his sore foot up on a chair and a sour look on his face. Mrs. Katz didn't stop scolding him until she had piled all the dinner plates into the sink, set out the coffee cups, cut into a banana pie and run out of breath.

"You've got your sweater on inside out," Harvey told her helpfully as soon as he could get a word in.

Mrs. Katz raised her arms and looked at the sleeves. All the little threads stuck out like wisps of hair. She stared blankly at her raised arms for a moment. Suddenly she smiled. "That's so," she said, and poured Mr. Katz some coffee.

"I didn't want to forget to tell you that Mr. Woolcott was here," she said to her husband.

"Woolcott?" said Mr. Katz. "I don't know any Woolcott."

"Well, you will when he comes back in thirty days," said Mrs. Katz.

"Thirty days?" said Mr. Katz. He looked at his watch. "We're going to be busy in thirty days, aren't we, Harvey?"

Harvey laughed.

"No you're not," said Mrs. Katz firmly. "Because Mr. Woolcott is a city housing inspector and he's coming back especially to see you."

Mr. Katz helped himself to another piece of pie. "I suppose he left a form for me to fill out. Inspectors are always leaving forms," he explained to Harvey.

"Not exactly," said Mrs. Katz. "This one he filled out himself. And he didn't call it a form, he called it a Litter Letter."

Mr. Katz took a big mouthful and answered at the same time. "Tell him he'll have to collect his litter someplace else. We don't have any."

"That," said Mrs. Katz, "is a matter of opinion."

Mr. Katz stopped eating to look at her.

"And in his opinion, you'd better do something about the garage."

Mr. Katz looked puzzled. "My garage? What's the garage have to do with it?"

Mrs. Katz took off her wrong-side-out sweater and

hung it on a hook at the side of the kitchen door. She stood at the door and said: "In the first place, it's so stuffed with junk, the garage doors won't close."

She walked over to the kitchen sink. "In the second place, it's a visual disturbance—that's what the man across the street complained to him about—a 'visual disturbance.' "

She moved across to the refrigerator. "In the third place, it's an 'unsightly mess' according to the woman down the block."

She went from the refrigerator over to the stove. "And in the fourth place, it turns the neighborhood into a junk yard, and"—she sat down in her chair at the table—"if you don't clean it up and put everything in order and keep the garage doors closed when not in use, you're going to be reported to the city clean-up department and they'll send their trucks over and haul everything to the dump and charge you for it."

"That's the fifth place," Harvey pointed out.

Mr. Katz half rose from his chair. "They will not!" he hollered.

Mrs. Katz smiled grimly. "Mr. Woolcott was *very* explicit. He not only has the complaints of every householder on this block, but he also has received a personal telephone call from the mayor, who is a relative of the lady who lives on the corner."

Mr. Katz sank into his chair with a little plop. "The mayor?"

"Well," said Mrs. Katz, "he happens to be her brother-in-law."

Mr. Katz began to yell. "Well, you can tell the mayor to butt out. You hear me!"

Harvey's ears popped.

"I told him I'd give you the message," she said calmly. She glanced around then, her eyes going first to the door, then to the sink, next to the refrigerator, from there to the stove, and then to the table at which they were seated, as she silently counted to five places on the fingers of her left hand. "I didn't forget anything," she said with pride.

Mr. Katz's face was turning pinker. "This is my property!" he hollered, "and no one is going to tell me what to do or not do on it."

"They already have," said Mrs. Katz and poured herself another cup of coffee.

"Well, I'm not cleaning out any garage to please the neighbors." He glowered at all the places in the kitchen. "Besides, I'm too busy."

Mrs. Katz snorted. "Busy," she said. "Busy filching rotten fruit from the supermarket dumpsters; that's what you've been busy at. It's a wonder that we all haven't been poisoned, what with you bringing home stale bread and old vegetables, and dented canned peas. It's a wonder," she said again as if she were just warming up to it, "that we all don't wake up dead in our beds."

Harvey finished his pie.

"I tell you I don't blame the neighbors. That's what I tell you. You just wait until they find out that the refrigerator is as full as the garage. Just wait. They'll probably send the health inspector and ask us to move out of the house."

"Nobody's going to take anything out of my garage," said Mr. Katz. "Nobody! Nobody's touching anything in that garage but me!"

"All you have to do," said Mrs. Katz softly, "is take everything out yourself and put it all back neatly. Stack everything, put things in boxes. Pile everything up, instead of leaving it all helter-skelter sticking out every which way. That's all you have to do."

Mr. Katz looked out the window at the side wall of his beloved garage. He looked at the stacks of window frames, old doors, secondhand gates and pieces of boards leaning against the wall. Slowly he began to smile and raised his bandaged foot. "I can't," he said.

"I can!" said Harvey.

Mr. Katz helped himself to another mouthful of pie and swallowed thoughtfully.

"It's not a job that can be done in a day," Mrs. Katz warned Harvey. "It might even take the rest of the summer."

"I don't mind," said Harvey quickly.

7

One is bun
Two is shoe
Three is tree
Four is door
Five is hive
Six are sticks
Seven is heaven
Eight is gate
Nine is line
Ten is hen

Before Harvey fell asleep that night he told himself that he'd better send postcards to his parents. With his eyes closed, he began to write them in his head.

Dear Mother: Dad and I are fine. Signed, *Harvey.*

Dear Dad: Mother and I are fine. Signed, *Harvey.*

For a moment he considered getting up and writing the cards out then, but after thinking about it for a while, he decided instead to write them first thing in the morning.

Sleepily he gazed at the rhyme tacked on the door. "One is bun. Two is shoe." He closed his eyes. "In the first place—" Mrs. Katz's voice seemed to be drifting through his head. He saw the frying pan on the floor in the front hall. He saw his postcards, already written and addressed, sitting in the frying pan. He wondered, dreamily, what his postcards were doing in the frying pan. They should be in the refrigerator, he thought, and fell asleep.

Harvey woke up the next morning feeling that there was something important he must do before he started helping Mr. Katz clean the garage. And he lay there staring at the slanted ceiling trying to remember what it was.

He heard the sound of Mr. and Mrs. Katz's voices coming up from the floor below as he jumped out of bed and went to the bathroom. Harvey got dressed and hurried down the stairs. His hand slid down the railing easily. It was a very solid railing and it felt smooth to his palm. It had come from an old house torn down for a new church, Mr. Katz had told him, and suddenly it seemed to Harvey to be the best-feeling railing he had ever had his hand on.

When he reached the bottom step, Harvey saw Mrs. Katz's old black frying pan sitting on the floor in front of the door. She must be going to the dentist, he thought, or maybe the beauty parlor today, and he stood there a moment looking at it.

Postcards! He remembered he was going to write postcards to his parents. Harvey ran back up the stairs, got the postcards, and wrote his messages. He put them into his pocket to mail and went down to breakfast.

It took Harvey a whole day to move enough things blocking the entrance to the garage to make room for him to get in. The next day Mr. Katz came out and sat on a kitchen chair on the driveway with his foot propped up on a stool, and directed the project. Every time Harvey pulled something out, Mr. Katz directed him to put it back in again. But when Mrs. Katz came out and hollered at him, he finally agreed to give some away.

"Can I have them?" said Harvey after he had made a neat stack of things on the driveway.

"Sure," said Mr. Katz, and Harvey took them upstairs to his room.

A few days later when the garage doors could be pulled back completely without bumping into bricks and two-by-fours and old cupboards, Harvey found something else.

"That's a Victrola," said Mr. Katz.

"A what?"

"An old-fashioned phonograph," he said.

"What's a phonograph?" said Harvey.

"An out-of-date record player."

"Oh," said Harvey, and laid it carefully on the grass. Suddenly he remembered the record player left behind in his bedroom in his parents' house. He remembered all the records stacked up on the shelves in his room. He remembered how he used to sit in the middle of his bed and listen to his favorite ones, and he turned away.

"You can have it if you want it," said Mrs. Katz. "It's nothing we're ever going to need."

"Thanks," said Harvey, and because she was standing there looking at him, he put all the pieces in an empty carton along with a bunch of dusty old records and carried it up to his room and shoved it under his cot. It would be handy to get at there, in case he ever wanted to listen to it.

Not long after, Mr. Katz gave him an old radio Harvey pulled out of a corner, and then he found a pair of earphones and a box of stuff with pieces of a telescope, and underneath that a porthole window.

"You might as well throw all that stuff away," Mr. Katz said with a sigh.

But it all seemed too good to throw away, so Harvey took it upstairs and piled it behind the sewing machine in one corner of his room.

"You want to keep that old pulley and long piece of rope?" he asked Mr. Katz a few days later when they had gotten to the shelves built on the inside of the back wall of the garage.

"I guess not," said Mr. Katz.

So Harvey took it.

It was beginning to get a little crowded in his room, but Harvey didn't care. When he woke up in the morning he no longer could see the doll in the birdcage. It was hidden by too many things. They were just the kinds of things Harvey thought he might need some day, in case he wanted to put up a tire swing, or make a shopping cart, or build a treehouse, or maybe a boat—or something like that.

"Everything's in," announced Harvey a few days later, "except one door."

Mr. Katz tried to squeeze it in. He pushed and he shoved, his face getting redder and redder. But there wasn't one spare foot of space for one more item. Everything just fit. Tightly. The garage door barely closed as it was.

"It won't fit," said Mr. Katz unhappily, standing back and wiping his face.

"You'll just have to haul it away," said Mrs. Katz.

"Oh no!" said Mr. Katz. "That's a good door!"

Harvey gazed at the door. It was an awfully nice door. "Don't worry about it," he said. "I'll take care of it."

Mr. Katz said, "Fine, put it someplace."

Mrs. Katz looked doubtful. "You're sure you have a place to put it?"

"Sure," said Harvey. "No trouble."

And when Mrs. Katz had gone off, he stuck the door on his back and carried it through the front door, up the stairs to his room.

"Where are you going to put it?" Mr. Katz stood behind him and peered in.

Harvey hoisted the door over everything and laid it flat on his bed. "I'll put it under my mattress," he said. "It would be a shame to waste such a good door."

Mr. Katz smiled.

"Better keep your door closed," he advised. There was a short pause. "That is, if you can close the door."

"Sure," said Harvey.

"Are you all finished with the garage cleaning?" Mrs. Katz asked when Harvey and Mr. Katz came into the kitchen.

"We will be," Mr. Katz said. "Soon as we fix the hole in the roof and the broken panel in the garage wall, and put in the automatic door opener."

"Now that'll be nice," said Mrs. Katz, probably thinking of the automatic door opener.

"I have to go downtown and pick up a few things first." Mr. Katz reached into his pocket and pulled out the Litter Letter. "Like nails," he said, turning it over. "And sandpaper." He continued reading from the list. "A pair of work gloves. A new handle for my hammer. Then while I'm about it I might as well get some new batteries for my flashlight. Well—I got some other stuff listed here, too." He gave the sheet of paper a flap.

"Whenever are you going to get the time to get all that?" Mrs. Katz was looking at the shopping list over his shoulder. "You've got an appointment with the dentist today—and you need a haircut."

Harvey looked over at the entryway. Sure enough, the frying pan was sitting there on the floor.

"That's so." Mr. Katz rubbed his hand over the back of his neck.

"Well, I guess Harvey and I can do your shopping for you. Can't we, Harvey?"

"Sure."

"Everything's down here on this list," said Mr. Katz.

Mrs. Katz sat down at the table and studied the list. Her lips moved as she began to read the items. "Bun," Harvey heard her mutter. Then "tree," but he figured he was mistaken.

"Excuse me," said Harvey. "I'll be right down." He dashed up the stairs and into his room. He had to climb over everything to reach the jacket he had left on his bed. It took him only a few minutes to return even counting a stop at the bathroom on the way down.

"All set?" said Mrs. Katz. She slung her handbag over her arm.

"All set," said Harvey. He glanced back to the diningroom table as he went out the front door. It wasn't until they were sitting on the bus and already halfway downtown that he remembered what he saw on the diningroom table as they were going out.

8

"The list!" Harvey shouted. "We forgot the list."

Mrs. Katz turned her head toward him. "Don't worry," she said, not at all upset.

"But we left it back there on the table."

"We'll remember it," she said unworriedly.

Harvey sat there while the bus turned the corner and tried to remember what was on the list. Haircut, was all he could recall, then he remembered that wasn't even on the list.

"Want to play a game?" asked Mrs. Katz.

"What kind of a game?" he asked unenthusiastically.

"It's easy. All you have to do is remember a rhyme."

Harvey said automatically, "I'm not very good at remembering."

She paid no attention to what he said. "One is bun," she began. "Two is shoe. That's easy enough, isn't it?"

Harvey heard himself snicker. "Oh, that rhyme."

"Three is tree," she went on.

"Four is door," said Harvey. "Five is hive. Six are sticks. Seven is heaven. Eight's a gate. Nine is line. And ten's a hen."

She seemed surprised.

"It's tacked on the back of my door," he said.

"That's because it's worth remembering," she said.

"I'm not very good at remembering," Harvey reminded her again.

"Well, you remembered that."

The bus came to a jolting stop. They got up and made their way to the door. They walked along the street together, Harvey frowning. "I wish we'd brought that list," he said, trying to remember the first item on it.

"All you have to remember is one is bun," said Mrs. Katz steering him across the street. "One is bun," she said again, pointing up.

"I don't see any bun," said Harvey looking up.

Mrs. Katz tapped at the side of her head. "Up here," she said. "You've got to see the bun up here."

Harvey sighed. "If you say so."

"Well, imagine it."

"Okay," said Harvey. He closed his eyes. He pictured a bun filled with a slice of hamburger oozing with ketchup. He saw melting cheese drizzling down the sides. It looked good. It looked awfully good.

"Got it?"

"I got it," said Harvey, his mouth beginning to water.

"Now picture it nailed shut with two-inch nails."

"You mean right through the cheese?" hollered Harvey. And he didn't want to, but he saw it anyway. Instantly.

"That'll do it," said Mrs. Katz and walked on.

"Who wants to eat a bun with nails in it?" grumbled Harvey, hurrying after her.

"Nails," said Mrs. Katz. "That was number one on the list. Connect it up with 'one is bun' and you won't forget it."

"Sure I will," grumbled Harvey. He followed her up the street to the next corner.

Mrs. Katz stopped. "Number two is shoe," she said.

Harvey looked around for the shoe store. "You going to get some new shoes?"

She shook her head. "One is bun, two is shoe," she quoted. "So now imagine you see a shoe."

"I can't," said Harvey quickly and just as quickly saw in his mind the old red tennis shoes Mrs. Katz wore around the house.

Mrs. Katz's eyes were closed. "The one I see has something odd about it."

Harvey grinned.

"I'm putting my foot into it," said Mrs. Katz.

"Ouch!" she said, opening her eyes wide.

"What's the matter?"

"It's lined with sandpaper."

Harvey laughed.

"Sandpaper," she said. "That was the second thing on the list. Two is shoe. I connected sandpaper with shoe and that's how I remembered it. Now for the third thing on the list."

"I can't remember anything more," said Harvey promptly.

"Three," she said firmly. "Three is tree. All you have to do is connect the third thing with tree."

Harvey sighed.

"The tree I see," she said, "has gloves growing on its branches. Because the third thing was canvas work gloves."

Harvey scratched his nose. He tried to picture a

tree. What came to his mind was the old maple tree at the corner of the school yard. He closed his eyes and instead of the tree he saw a big glove growing there with the fingers sticking up and out. He saw little kids at recess climbing the glove and sitting between the fingers.

"Three is canvas gloves," she said and walked along so briskly that Harvey had to run to keep up.

"I know, I know," said Harvey.

"Hammer," she said, when they came to the next corner. "That's the fourth item. I remembered it because four is door and the door I see in my head has a big hole smashed through it."

"Four is door," said Harvey as the picture of the Katzes' front door with a hammer smashing a hole into it sprang to his mind.

Mrs. Katz closed her eyes again. "Five is hive. The one in my head is buzzing with Christmas tree lights."

"Christmas tree lights?" said Harvey. He looked at her doubtfully. One thing he was sure of was that Mr. Katz hadn't had any Christmas tree lights on his list.

"All blinking," Mrs. Katz said, blinking at him.

"Batteries!" said Harvey. But his elation didn't last long.

They crossed the street to the hardware store. "You go in here," instructed Mrs. Katz, "and get the first five items on the list, and I'll go to the department store across the street for the next five." She rummaged through her purse and gave him some money.

Harvey suddenly began to feel a little sick. "I'm not very good at remembering," he shouted after her. But she merely waved as she hurried across with the light.

Harvey stood in front of the hardware store and wished he had remembered to bring the list. Mrs. Katz had reached the other side of the street. "One is bun!" she hollered across at him.

Slowly Harvey went through the entrance of the hardware store. "One is bun," he muttered. The picture of a bun dripping with cheese filled his mind. The vision of nails sticking right through it made him shudder.

"May I help you?" asked the hardware clerk.

"Nails," said Harvey. "I want some two-inch nails."

"Anything else?" asked the clerk after he had plucked a handful from a bin and dropped them into a sack.

"Two is shoe," said Harvey.

65

"We don't carry shoes," said the clerk.

Mrs. Katz's red tennis shoes appeared in Harvey's mind. He saw her trying to put her foot into one—"Sandpaper," he said.

"What next?" The clerk tossed the package onto the counter next to the nails.

Three, thought Harvey. Three is tree. In his mind's eye he saw the kids sitting between the fingers of the big cotton glove growing in the school yard. And he picked out the extra-large size from the glove rack. Four is door, he mumbled, and saw in his head the Katzes' smashed front door. "Hammer," he said.

He grinned while waiting for the batteries, thinking of the beehive buzzing with Christmas tree lights, and then he proudly carried the bag full of five items out of the store.

On the way back Harvey practiced spelling the street names backwards, and when they got off the bus, he swaggered along beside Mrs. Katz, feeling sharp as a tack.

"Summer's almost over," said Mrs. Katz as they reached the front door. "I guess your parents will be expecting you home soon."

Harvey stopped. He gazed at the mismatched windows and the big front church door and the wooden chimney and everything suddenly turned blurry as a lump rose in his throat.

Mr. Katz was pounding on the roof of the garage when Harvey came down out of the house with all his things stuffed into a paper bag. He couldn't find his duffle bag.

"Oh Harvey!" called Mr. Katz. He stopped hammering.

"Yes?" said Harvey, his voice cracking a little.

"You remember where you got those nails?"

"Sure," said Harvey.

"Well, I sure could use about a quarter's worth more." He stuck his hand in his pocket and tossed Harvey a coin.

"Okay," said Harvey.

He wasted no time. He went down to the hardware store and came back with the nails. His paper bag was still sitting on the bottom porch step waiting for him.

Mr. Katz came down from the roof. Mrs. Katz opened the back door. Good smells drifted out.

Mr. Katz turned around and sniffed.

"What are you doing?" Harvey asked Mrs. Katz as he picked up his bag from the step.

"Celebrating," said Mrs. Katz. "The inspector

just left. I showed him everything," she said proudly, "outside and in."

"My room?" said Harvey. "You showed him my room!"

"I tried to, but for some reason I couldn't open the door."

"Oh" said Harvey in a weak voice. "That's too bad."

"What's in the oven?" Mr. Katz's head was raised. He sniffed at the air.

"Your favorite cake," said Mrs. Katz.

"Cake?" said Harvey, sniffing too. "What kind of cake?"

Mr. Katz was breathing deeply, his eyes closed, his hands folded over his stomach. "Chocolate cheese-cake," he said between breaths.

"I only make it for special occasions," explained Mrs. Katz.

Harvey closed his eyes too. He took a long deep breath. What he smelled was like nothing he had ever smelled before. Reluctantly, he opened his eyes. He picked up his paper sack. "Well, I guess I'd better be going," he said.

"Not before you have a piece of this cake!" declared Mrs. Katz.

It was chocolatey and cheesey and high as the

evening star. It was flavorful and toothsome and full of dumpster eggs and dumpster butter and dumpster cream, and Mr. Katz and Harvey ate every last chocolatey cheesey crumb and would have eaten more if they could.

"I think if I had to choose what I wanted for the last meal I'd ever have on earth, it would end with chocolate cheesecake," said Mr. Katz, lolling back in his chair.

"Me too," said Harvey, gasping a little. "As a matter of fact," he said, pushing his chair back to make more room for his stomach, "I think I'm ready to die right now."

And that's when the front doorbell rang.

9

"I'll get it," said Harvey, and full of chocolate cheesecake, he slowly made his way to the front door. The doorbell rang again before he got there. He put his hand on the big knob and pulled. The door opened.

There stood his mother and his father. Behind them was a policeman.

"We're looking for—" began his mother, and then she bent and peered at him. "Harvey?"

"Harvey!" said his father.

And they stood there a moment gaping at each other.

"Harvey darling!" his mother shrieked, and hugged him.

"Harvey," his father said again and clasped him to his neat striped sport shirt.

"Harvey, you're fat!" said his mother, and then they both began talking at once.

His father said, "You told me you were staying with your mother!" His mother said, "You told me you were going to stay with your father!"

Harvey couldn't think of anything to say.

"What did you say your name was?" Mr. Katz was staring owlishly at Harvey's father.

"Bean. This is our son and his name is Harvey Bean." He glared at the Katzes.

"How do you do," said Mrs. Katz to Harvey's parents.

The police officer cleared his throat. But Mr. Bean didn't give him a chance to speak. "Now look here, officer," he said in the sharp voice he always used when warning the paperboy not to throw the paper on the roof again. "It's obvious that something funny has been going on here. What is my son doing with these people?"

"Katz," said Mr. Katz calmly. "Our name is Katz."

"Katz?" said the officer. "Aren't you the one who's always stirring up the garbage down at the supermarket dumpster?"

"Who? Me?" said Mr. Katz. "I don't stir up any

garbage. I merely take what's too good to be thrown away."

"It's not stealing," Harvey said quickly. "There's no law against taking something someone has thrown away."

"That's so," said the officer.

"You scavenger!" Harvey's father shouted. "You stole my son!"

Mr. Katz's pink cheeks got pinker. His cap fell off his head. "I didn't steal him. I found him. At the dumpster."

"You found Harvey in the garbage?" Mrs. Bean said in a strangled voice.

"You might put it that way," Mr. Katz said with an accusing stare. "And I didn't kidnap him. I just invited him home for dinner."

"And he stayed." Mrs. Katz put her hand on Harvey's shoulder and squeezed.

His mother gasped.

"He could have left anytime," said Mr. Katz.

"Anytime." Mrs. Katz nodded her head.

"I didn't want to go," said Harvey.

Harvey's father seemed to have lost the thread of the inquiry. "What do you mean, you found him at the dumpster?"

"I brought him home," said Mr. Katz.

"Along with a hundred pounds of rotten tomatoes," said Mrs. Katz.

"Tomatoes?" said Harvey's mother.

"I hate to see good things go to waste," explained Mr. Katz. "They were just a little overripe."

"Whatever did you do with all those tomatoes?" Harvey's mother asked Mrs. Katz.

"Pickled some. Stewed some. Made relish. And soups and sauces and gravies."

"And spaghetti!" said Harvey.

Mr. Katz said proudly, "My wife can make a gourmet dish out of a half-rotten potato."

"I just use the good part," said Mrs. Katz modestly.

Harvey saw a look of bewilderment come over his father's face. "Tomatoes?" his father demanded. "Potatoes! What has that to do with my son!"

Mr. Katz turned to stare at him. It seemed, Harvey knew, perfectly clear and simple to Mr. Katz.

Mrs. Katz stepped between them. "I'll tell you."

The police officer got out his notebook as if he were getting ready for a confession. Harvey's father crossed his arms over his chest as if he were a judge.

"My husband is no child-snatcher. He's a saving man. He can't bear to see any good thing go to waste. No matter if it's only half a melon, or a scrap of a boy."

Harvey's mother began to cry.

"You should have let us know where you were," his father said.

"I did," said Harvey. "I sent you each a postcard."

"A postcard?" said his father.

"I didn't receive any postcard," said his mother.

Harvey put his hands in his pockets. Slowly he pulled out two crumpled pieces and stared at them. "I guess I forgot to mail them."

Suddenly his mother laughed. "You never were very good at remembering things," she said and wiped her eyes.

Mrs. Katz put her two soft hands on Harvey's shoulders. "We don't mind keeping him," she said. "If it's all right with you, we'd like him to stay with us—if he wants to."

"I want him to come home with me," said Harvey's mother. "I missed him."

"I want Harvey to live with me," Harvey's father said without clearing his throat or waiting to think it over.

The officer's gaze moved from Mr. and Mrs. Katz to Mr. and Mrs. Bean.

"Well, Harvey, what do you want?"

Harvey's heart began to beat joyfully. His parents wanted him. Even if they were going to stay separated they still wanted him. They wanted him, maybe, almost as much as Mr. and Mrs. Katz did. He stood there feeling blissful. It was even better than feeling full of chocolate cheesecake.

"Harvey?" whispered his mother as if she couldn't stand to wait any longer.

Harvey came to his decision. "I could live with you," he said to his mother, "on school days—and go stay with Dad on the weekends. If you're not too busy," he said to his father.

His father smiled.

Harvey heard Mrs. Katz give a long quivering sob.

"Could I come back and stay here with you next summer?" he said to her. She wrapped her arms around him and gave him a hug, and his father shook hands with Mr. Katz, and Mrs. Katz opened the door and said goodby to the police officer.

"We won't touch anything in your room," Mr. Katz promised Harvey, and winked at him.

"You can take anything you want home with you," said Mrs. Katz, smiling happily.

"Can I?" Harvey turned to his mother. "Can I take anything?"

His mother smiled at Mrs. Katz over Harvey's

head. "Of course," she said.

Harvey took the door he had stashed away under his mattress.

"You sure you know what you're going to do with this door?" his father asked as he helped Mr. Katz tie it to the top of Harvey's mother's car.

"Sure," said Harvey quickly.

"Goodby!" said Mrs. Katz and gave him another hug.

His mother waved to Mr. and Mrs. Katz from the driver's seat.

"Goodby! Goodby!" Harvey shouted.

"Just a minute!" hollered Mrs. Katz. And they all waited with the motor running while she ran into the house and came out again a minute later. She was breathless. In her hand was a sheet of paper with words on it.

"One is bun," she whispered to Harvey, sticking her head through the car window.

"I'll frame it and hang it in my room!" Harvey hollered at her as the car began to move. And then they turned the corner, and the familiar house with its wooden chimney and patchwork windows was out of sight.

They dropped his father off in front of his apartment.

"Tomorrow is the first day of school," his mother said as they proceeded up the street.

Harvey stared out the window. They passed his school and he looked right through the walls into his classroom and saw the teacher's frowning face and the grins of his classmates. All of a sudden he could hear the snickers and the laughter.

"I don't feel so good," he said to his mother.

She glanced at him. "Something you ate," she said bobbing her head wisely. "I'm going to give you some Pepto-Bismol as soon as we get home."

10

"Harvey Bean!"

The voice banged at Harvey's ears. He had arrived at school all right that morning. He had put his lunch bag in the new locker, found the new classroom, sat down in the new seat and smiled at Cindy Wescott sitting in the desk next to him. She had not smiled back.

He didn't like her anyway, he told himself. He didn't like the new teacher much better. When she had come into the room and told them her name, he had thought of a giant-sized soft drink bottle with a polka-dotted scarf tied around its neck.

Harvey opened his eyes. The teacher was staring at him.

"Are you paying attention?"

"Sure," mumbled Harvey.

She eyed him suspiciously. "What did I say?"

"You said your name was Sprite," Harvey said, surprised that he had remembered.

"*Ms.* Sprite," she corrected.

Jonathan Andrews held up his hand. "I busted my pencil."

"Well, sharpen it Jonathan," the teacher said. And she waited until he had clumped to the sharpener, whirred the pencil to a sharp point, and returned to his seat.

"Eyes front, please," she said to everyone and looked at Harvey.

Then she turned her back and began writing on the blackboard. She wrote: COPY and MEMORIZE across the top of the board. Next she wrote: OUR COUNTRY'S EARLY INDUSTRIES. Then she made a column of numbers from 1 to 10 and started to write a word next to each number, saying the number and the word as she wrote it down.

"Number one," she said loudly, "is LUMBERING."

Everyone began busily writing, copying in their notebooks the list Ms. Sprite was putting on the blackboard. Everyone, that is, but Harvey.

"Number one is bun," Harvey was thinking. And he was seeing a hamburger on a bun with an order of French fries, only instead of potatoes he saw sticks of lumber.

"Number two is FISHING," said Ms. Sprite as she wrote it on the board.

"Number two is shoe," Harvey said to himself as he sat with his hands folded. He closed his eyes and saw a shoe dangling on the end of a fishing line.

"Number three, WHALING," said Ms. Sprite, writing as fast as she could. Harvey could hear the sound of the chalk against the blackboard.

"Number three is tree," thought Harvey and saw a whale climbing a tree.

When Ms. Sprite said, "Number four is TOBACCO GROWING," Harvey thought of the Katzes' big front door standing in the middle of a tobacco plantation.

When she said, "SAWMILLING is Number seven," Harvey said in his head, "Seven is heaven," and saw sawdust raining down from the sky. When she said, "FUR TRAPPING is Number ten," Harvey said, "Ten is hen," and almost laughed aloud at the sudden vision of a chicken in a fur coat.

He was still sitting there with his eyes closed grinning at the picture in his head when he felt the sudden silence around him. He peered through his eyelashes.

Ms. Sprite was standing, her arms folded, facing the class.

"Harvey!"

Harvey opened his eyes wide.

"This is not your nap time," she said. "And you are supposed to be paying attention."

The class laughed.

"I am paying attention," Harvey said.

The teacher smiled sourly. "Well suppose you tell us what you were paying attention to."

The class laughed even louder. Cindy Wescott's eyes were fastened on him expectantly. Jonathan Andrews was smirking.

"He hasn't written anything down on his paper!" Jonathan reported loudly, looking over Harvey's shoulder.

"I don't have to," Harvey said just as loudly. "I memorized it without writing it down."

Cindy Wescott giggled.

Ms. Sprite rapped on her desk edge so hard with her pencil that it broke into pieces and flew into the air. She held up her hand and waited for complete silence.

"Has everyone finished copying the memory work?" She was speaking to the whole class but everyone knew she meant Harvey.

81

SISKIYOU COUNTY SCHOOLS LIBRARY

Harvey didn't say anything.

Ms. Sprite turned around and erased the writing on the board. Then she faced the class and smiled slowly. It squeezed out, spreading like honey across her face. "All right, Harvey," she said in a slightly sticky voice, "let us have a demonstration of your amazing memory."

Harvey stood up. "One is bun," he said. And then he had to wait for everyone to stop laughing.

He thought of the bun and he thought of the French fries made of lumber.

"Number one is LUMBERING," he said, and no one laughed. He went right on. He recited the whole list from Number 1 to Number 10. He recited them in the right order and made no mistakes It was easy. All he had to do was say the number, think of the rhyming word and let the picture he had connected with it pop up all by itself. He could have recited the list backwards just as easily. And for good measure he did. Then triumphantly he sat down.

"Well, how was the first day of school?" his mother asked when he got home.

Harvey thought of the teacher almost fainting with surprise at his amazing memory. He thought of the astonished faces of his classmates. He thought of Cindy Wescott looking at him with admiration.

Harvey shrugged. "It was okay," he said and smiled all the way up to his room.

His mother followed him up the stairs. She came into his room after him and stood for a moment looking at the door leaning against his wall.

"What on earth did you want to take that door home with you for?" she said.

The door. Harvey gazed at the door. What was it he had wanted it for? Harvey scratched his head. The last day of summer seemed far behind him. He couldn't remember.

"You mean you carted that door all the way home and you don't even know what for?"

"Well, you can't expect me to remember everything," Harvey said.